Caching In

Kristin Butcher

Orca currents

WITHDRAWN

ORCA BOOK PUBLISHERS

Library and Archives Canada Cataloguing in Publication

Butcher, Kristin
Caching in / Kristin Butcher.
(Orca currents)

Issued also in electronic formats.
ISBN 978-1-4598-0233-9 (bound).--ISBN 978-1-4598-0232-2 (pbk.)

I. Title. II. Series: Orca currents
PS8553.U6972C33 2013   jc813'.54   C2012-907471-3

First published in the United States, 2013
Library of Congress Control Number: 2012952953

Summary: Eric and his best friend, Chris, find themselves
on a high-stakes geocaching treasure hunt.

MIX
Paper from
responsible sources
FSC
www.fsc.org   FSC® C016245

*Orca Book Publishers is dedicated to preserving the environment and has
printed this book on Forest Stewardship Council® certified paper.*

Orca Book Publishers gratefully acknowledges the support for its
publishing programs provided by the following agencies: the Government
of Canada through the Canada Book Fund and the Canada Council for the Arts,
and the Province of British Columbia through the BC Arts Council
and the Book Publishing Tax Credit.

The author gratefully acknowledges the financial support provided by the
BC Arts Council during the writing of this book.

Cover photography by Getty Images
Author photo by Steve Loughead

ORCA BOOK PUBLISHERS
PO Box 5626, Stn. B
Victoria, BC Canada
V8R 6S4

ORCA BOOK PUBLISHERS
PO Box 468
Custer, WA USA
98240-0468

www.orcabook.com
Printed and bound in Canada.

16 15 14 13 • 4 3 2 1

*For Diane Swanson, with thanks
for introducing me to geocaching.*

Chapter One

Chris and I duck behind a tree and hope the group of people up ahead hasn't seen us.

"Dearly beloved," we hear. "We are gathered here today, in the presence of these witnesses, to join this man and this woman in holy matrimony. Marriage is a commitment not to be entered into unadvisedly or lightly, but reverently and solemnly. It is—"

"Jeez, man! Are you kidding me?" Chris peers around the tree. He's not exactly whispering. "It's a wedding!"

I haul him back. "Shut up. Somebody will hear you."

"It's a freakin' wedding!" Chris exclaims again, without turning down the volume.

"I can see that," I say.

"But this is a cemetery! Who gets married in a cemetery?"

"Them, obviously."

"But why? Tell me why, Eric. It's a cemetery!"

"How the heck should I know?" I growl through gritted teeth. "Why don't you yell a little louder and ask them?"

Finally, he gets the message. But Chris is not what you'd call patient.

After a few minutes, he flops against the tree and grumbles, "I didn't sign up to spend the afternoon at a freakin' wedding."

I pull my GPS from my pocket and check the screen. "Well, we don't have a lot of choice. According to the coordinates, the cache is on the other side of those people, so we wait for them to finish their wedding, or we come back later." Then I add, "And hope nobody gets there before us."

It's that last bit that convinces Chris to stay. If someone were to beat us to that cache, it would eat him alive.

Chris and I started geocaching about a year ago after I read an article about it. It was something different to do, and all we needed was a GPS. So we went to the website and joined up. The longitude and latitude coordinates for the hidden caches were right there. All we had to do was load them into our GPS and go where they took us.

Geocaching is kind of like hunting for treasure. Not that the stuff in the caches is all that great. Usually they are filled with plastic toys and other junk like that, but it doesn't matter. We have a good time just hunting for them and reading the logbook to see who's been there before us. Sometimes we take whatever is inside and replace it with something else, but mostly we just add our names to the log and put the cache back where we found it.

The better we get at geocaching, though, the bigger the challenge we want. Lately, we've started focusing on caches with puzzles and clues and lots of twists. And ones that nobody else has discovered yet. Being the first names in a cache's logbook is important—especially to Chris.

I glance sideways at him. He's totally zoned into his phone. I don't know if he's texting someone or playing a game, but he's quiet. That's all I care about.

Though I don't say so, I feel dumb hiding behind a tree in a cemetery. It's not the sort of place fifteen-year-old guys hang out on a Saturday afternoon—unless they're planning to rob a grave or something. I think about what to do if someone sees us. Beat it out of there, I guess. The geocaching rules are pretty clear about making sure nobody spots you opening a cache.

At last we hear applause. Chris and I peer around the tree in time to see the bride and groom kiss.

Then the wedding guests start hugging the bride and thumping the groom on the back. Cameras are clicking all over the place as people take turns getting their pictures taken with the newlyweds. Everyone is smiling so hard, you'd think they were in a toothpaste commercial.

The bride and groom pose by one of the headstones, and then the bride crouches down and sets her bouquet on the grass in front of it. She's crying. One of the guests passes her a tissue. She dabs at her eyes and smiles. The groom helps her up. She buries her head in his shoulder.

A few minutes later, the whole wedding group starts moving away down the path.

"It's about time," Chris mutters as he stuffs his phone into his jeans. "I thought they were never gonna leave."

He starts to step away from the tree, but I yank him back.

"Not yet."

We wait until all the people have gotten into their cars and the last one has driven away.

"Okay." I take one last look around to make sure the coast is clear. "Let's go."

The GPS leads us right to the spot where the wedding was.

"This is it," I tell Chris. "Now we find the cache."

We start looking around. The area is mostly grass and graves, though there are a couple of trees and a flower bed too.

Chris starts tromping through the flowers, using his foot to search between the plants.

"Take it easy!" I tell him. "We don't want to wreck the place. Besides, the cache has to be in plain sight."

"Whatever," he mumbles, but he stops kicking the flowers. After a while he says, "Hey, Eric. Are you sure this is the spot? I don't see a freakin' thing that looks like a cache."

I check the GPS again. "This is it, man."

He frowns. "Maybe you copied the coordinates down wrong."

I shake my head. "I didn't."

But I begin to doubt myself. I was excited when I saw the new cache listing on the website this morning. I called Chris right away. In my rush to get searching, I could have screwed up the numbers.

"So where is it?" Chris demands.

I do another scan of the area. Headstone, headstone, headstone, bouquet. I walk over to the bouquet. I don't know why. It couldn't possibly be the cache. But there is nowhere else to look.

I kneel down for a closer look. It's just a bunch of flowers and ribbons. That's all. Wait a second. Something is stuffed in the middle of the flowers. It's yellow and white, like the flowers, so it's a wonder I even noticed it. I pull it out.

It's a small cardboard box—the kind medicine comes in, but it's been painted.

And there's printing on one side. CACHE.

"I got it!" I holler, though Chris is now standing right beside me.

"Open it up," he says.

"It doesn't feel like there's anything inside."

"Quit talkin' and open the stupid thing!" Like I said before, Chris is not real patient.

I open the flap and tip the box. Out slides an egg.

Chris scowls. "That's it? That's all that's in there?" He grabs the box from me, shakes it and looks inside. "So where's the log? There's supposed to be a log. How can we prove we're the first ones to find the cache if there's no log?"

"Sign our names on the box and write down the date and time," I suggest.

He fishes a pen from his pocket, but I can tell he's ticked off. Chris believes in playing by the rules. And the rules say there's supposed to be a log. When he's finished, he puts out his hand for the egg. I don't give it to him. Instead, I shake it and hold it up to my eye.

"It's been hollowed out," I say. "See the hole?"

"So what? Just put it back in the cache, and let's get out of here."

"There's something inside."

Suddenly, Chris is interested. "What?"

"I don't know. But whatever it is, it went in through that little hole." I shake the egg again. "There's no way it's coming back out though."

Chris sticks out his hand. "Let me see that. I can get it out."

I pass him the egg.

He brings his eye to the hole. "Yup. There's something in there, all right."

"How are you going to get it out?"

"Easy," he says. Then he smacks the egg against the headstone.

Chapter Two

A scrap of paper flutters to the ground. Chris makes a dive for it, but I scoop it up first.

"What is it?" He lunges for the paper again, but I hold it out of his reach.

"Hang on." I frown and squint at the tiny writing. "It's an obituary."

"That figures!" he hoots.

Even though I should be used to Chris's eruptions—we've been friends since kindergarten—I jump. Being in a graveyard is starting to creep me out.

"It makes perfect sense, right?" he adds sarcastically. "I mean, what with us being in a cemetery and all." Then he shakes his head. "This geocache keeps getting weirder and weirder. So whose obituary is it?" He spreads his arms to take in the nearby graves. "One of the locals?"

I peer at the headstone in front of me—the one with the bouquet. "Actually, yeah," I say. "It's this guy right here. Richard Carlisle."

Chris looks at the headstone and then over my shoulder at the obituary. "Richard Carlisle? That's the dead guy's name?"

"Yeah. You know him?"

I expect a wisecrack in reply, but to my surprise Chris says, "I'm not sure."

My jaw drops open. "Are you serious? You *know* this guy?"

"Not personally, but I definitely know the name."

"From where?"

He scowls. "I can't remember." Then he points to the scrap of paper. "Read the obituary. Maybe it says something that will trigger my memory."

I start to read.

CARLISLE, RICHARD CAMERON

Forty-eight-year-old Richard Carlisle lost his battle with cancer on March 26 at 3:00 PM in the north wing of the Royal Jubilee Hospital. His loving daughter, Jane, was by his side.

Richard was born and raised in West Vancouver. After earning a degree in commerce at UBC, he took over the family business, moving the main office to Victoria.

Always up for a new adventure, Richard's favorite saying was "1, 2, 3—go!" His biggest challenge and greatest success was his company. At the time of his death, it was valued at over $19 million.

He was predeceased by his wife and parents and will be greatly missed by all who knew him. No service by request. In lieu of flowers, donations may be made to the Tree of Life, 31 Richmond Road.

"So?" I say when I'm finished. "Do you remember how you know this guy?"

Chris's mouth hardens into a tight line, and he shakes his head.

"Maybe you heard his name on television or read it in the paper," I suggest. "The obituary says he was rich, so he's probably been in the news."

He shakes his head again. "I don't think that's it."

"Too bad there isn't a picture. That might help you remember."

Chris holds out his hand for the obituary.

"What?" I snicker. "You think reading it yourself is going to make a difference?"

He doesn't even let on that he heard me. He just waggles his fingers for the obituary. I sigh and hand it over.

After a couple of minutes, he says, "What are the dates on the headstone?"

I look at the marker. "January 15, 1960, to March 4, 2012."

Chris frowns. "That doesn't make any sense."

"Why?"

"Well, it says here that Carlisle was forty-eight when he died."

"So?"

He looks up from the obituary. "Do the math. If he was born in 1960 and he died in 2012, that would make him fifty-two, *not* forty-eight."

I shrug. "Maybe the person who wrote the obituary isn't very good at subtraction, or the guy who engraved the headstone got the birthdate wrong."

"The year he was born *and* the day he died? The obituary says Carlisle died on the twenty-sixth, and the headstone says the fourth. Another screwup? More bad math?" Chris looks back at the scrap of paper.

"So what are you saying?"

He rolls his eyes like he's explaining something to a two-year-old. "This is supposed to be a challenging cache, right?"

I nod.

"Well, if you ask me, so far it's been a bust. We followed the coordinates and found the cache. So where's the challenge in that? Unless—" he pauses for so long that I'm ready to stick my hand down his throat for the rest of the sentence "—the obituary is a clue to another cache."

I scramble to my feet and read the notice again. If there's a clue in there, I sure don't see it.

"So what's the clue?" I demand.

Chris's face relaxes, and his eyes start to glitter. He looks like a cat that just ate every fish in the aquarium. He knows I'm dying of curiosity, and he's obviously getting a charge out of torturing me.

I punch him in the arm. "Get on with it, Einstein!"

He laughs, but at least he starts to explain. "I think the longitude and latitude coordinates for the next cache are hidden in the obituary. That's why Carlisle's age is wrong. Forty-eight is the first part of every latitude coordinate around Victoria. And that's why the date of death is wrong too. It needs to be the twenty-sixth because that's part of a coordinate.

"Here." He whips his pen and a crumpled paper from his pocket and pushes them at me. "Let's read the obituary again. As we pick out the coordinates, you write them down."

So we do. Once we know what we're looking for, it's easy.

"What have we got?" Chris asks when we're finished.

"Forty-eight degrees 26 minutes 3 seconds North, and 123 degrees 19 minutes 31 seconds West."

"All right!" Chris grins and gives me a high five. "Plug those bad boys into the GPS and let's get going." He starts jogging down the path toward our bikes.

"Wait," I holler at him. "We have to put this cache back."

He does a quick turnaround. "Oh, yeah. Right. I forgot."

"*And,* since we broke the egg, we have to stick something of our own into the cache too."

Chris lowers his head and squints at me. "That means we can take the obituary, right?"

"Yeah, but if we do, nobody else can get the next clue."

Chris grins. "I know."

I shake my head. "Where's the fun in that? We already have the lead, and you can take a picture of the obituary with your phone in case we need to look at it again."

A scowl replaces the grin. "You know, Eric, you can be a real downer sometimes."

"You're the one who wanted a challenge," I remind him.

He doesn't say anything. How can he? I'm right.

"So," I continue, "what are we going to stash in the cache? Your pen?"

"Forget it!" He snatches it from my hand and shoves it into his pocket. "Put something of *yours* in the cache."

"Why? You're the one who broke the egg. Besides"—I start picking through my pockets—"the only thing I have is this ticket to last night's school dance."

"Perfect," Chris says, plucking the black-and-green strip from my fingers. "It's worth way more than that hollowed-out egg." He checks the stamp on the back. "At least, it was before you used it." Then his face lights up. "Maybe it'll confuse the next guys who find the cache. They won't know if the clue is the ticket or the obituary. They might end up at our school!" He finds the idea so funny that he chuckles the whole time he's stuffing the cache back inside the bouquet.

Chapter Three

Plugging longitude and latitude into the GPS is pretty much the same as punching in an address. A map appears on the screen, and the guy inside the GPS—we call our dude Merlin—gives us directions to our destination. He doesn't always pick the shortest route. If you're riding a bike, this can mean a lot of pedaling. It would be way better if he told us where we were supposed to go—say, the Inner Harbor or Beacon Hill Park. Even if he told us which part of town we were headed for, it would help. But he doesn't. We never know until we get there.

And even then, Merlin only takes us so far. It would be cool if he said the cache was behind a bench or inside a hollow log. But no. He hasn't been programmed for that little trick, so once we get close, Merlin signs off and Chris and I are on our own.

It's my GPS, so I lead the way—for the first half hour, anyway. But as soon as I wheel onto Richmond Road, Chris shoots past me and speeds away.

"Hey!" I holler after him. "Where are you going?"

"Where do you think?" he yells over his shoulder.

I have no clue, but Chris is already half a block ahead, so I have to pedal hard to catch up. The street is narrow, and there are parked cars on both sides, so we're pretty much riding in the middle of traffic. A couple of cars honk. Chris gives them the finger.

When we get to the light at Richmond Road and Bay Street, Chris swings into the turn lane. I look at the GPS mounted on my handlebars.

"In one hundred meters, turn left to destination," Merlin says.

"Hmph," I mumble in amazement as I follow Chris through the intersection.

And just like that, we're in the parking lot of the Royal Jubilee Hospital.

I brake and lower one foot to the pavement. "This is it."

But Chris doesn't stop. He hangs another left and coasts down an incline and through the entrance to the parkade. I follow him.

We slide our bikes into the bike rack and lock them. "How did you know we were gonna end up at the hospital?" I say. "And how did you know these bike racks were here?"

He taps the side of his head with his finger. "Brains."

"I'm serious, man."

Chris frowns. "What? You think I'm not smart?"

"Yeah, you're a genius. Now answer the question."

He shrugs. "I played a hunch. When you turned onto Richmond Road, I automatically thought, hospital. I mean, what other landmarks are on the street? Then I remembered the obituary. It said Carlisle died here. I figured it was a clue. As for the bike rack, I used it last summer when my grandfather was having surgery."

I nod and glance around. "So where do we start looking?"

We head back into the sunshine and up to the main driveway.

Chris points to the shrubbery surrounding the parkade. "What about there?"

I shake my head. "I don't think so. There aren't any weeds. And the shrubs are all perfectly trimmed. The hospital obviously has a gardener. If the cache was hidden in there, he would have found it. Besides, cars are constantly whizzing up and down the road and turning into the hospital parking lot. Somebody would see us finding the cache—just like they would have seen whoever hid it."

"Unless it was hidden in the middle of the night."

I shoot Chris a dirty look. "If you're thinking what I think you're thinking, forget it. We're not coming back here later."

"Fine," he concedes grudgingly.

We take the crosswalk to a bench on the opposite sidewalk. As we flop down, I sigh and Chris boots a pebble.

"So now what?" he says. "It can't be in the middle of the road."

I shake my head. "No."

Even so, we both stare at the driveway as if the cache is going to magically pop out of the pavement. Gradually, my gaze shifts to the hospital. There's a sandwich place attached to it, and as a steady stream of people walks in and then out with subs, my stomach starts to growl. Lunch was hours ago.

Chris pulls out his phone and presses a few buttons.

"Tree of Life," he mutters. There's a determination in his voice that makes me forget about sandwiches.

"What?"

"That's the clue."

"What clue?"

"Look there." He points to a sprawling tree a little to our left. It's not tall, but it's really wide, and its branches are all bent over. The leaves practically touch the ground. "What do you see?"

"A tree."

"A tree of life?"

I feel my eyebrows dive into one another. "What are you talking about?"

He taps his phone. "The obituary said that instead of giving flowers, people should donate to the Tree of Life. So I did a search. There's a *Tree of Life* movie and a Tree of Life store. Why would the dead guy's family want people to donate to those? And there is nothing on Richmond Road. It's gotta be a clue."

We stand up and head for the tree.

The dangling leaves form a thick, green, circular curtain. We push through, and suddenly the parkade, driveway and hospital disappear. We can't see out, and nobody can see in.

The tree looks ancient. The bark is black and cracked, and the branches are all knobbly and gnarled. If a tree can get arthritis, this one definitely has it.

"Hey, look!" Chris nudges me and points above our heads. "It's a knothole."

I nod. "I see it. There's another one too—a couple of feet above that one. Do you think that's where the cache is?"

Chris takes a deep breath and steps up to the tree. "We'll soon find out."

Like I said, the tree isn't tall, but Chris is, so he has no trouble reaching the lower knothole. When he stands on his toes, he can even feel inside.

I hold my breath as he gropes around.

"Well?" I say when he finally pulls his hand out.

He makes a face and wipes his hand on his jeans. "Nothin'. I should've known that was too easy."

"But that's good, right? Less chance that anybody's found the cache yet. We'll be the first ones."

Chris shakes his head. "Or not, since I can't reach that high, there are no branches to climb, and I don't seem to have a ladder."

I ignore the sarcasm. "I can stand on your shoulders," I say. I'm shorter than Chris and lighter too.

He doesn't answer right away. He hates it when somebody else comes up with an idea. Finally, he nods and mumbles, "It could work." Then he crouches on his knees in front of the tree.

I hop onto his shoulders and grab the trunk as he stands up. The knothole is right at my eye level. And there's something inside—a metal tube with plastic caps on both ends. I reach in and grab it.

"I've got it!" I call down to Chris.

In a matter of seconds, I'm back on the ground, and the two of us are scrambling to get the tube open.

"It's a paper," Chris announces as he fishes it out.

"Another clue, I bet."

As he unrolls the paper, his eyes practically pop out of his head.

"What? What is it?" I demand, yanking on his arm so I can see too.

I blink a couple of times to make sure I'm not hallucinating. The paper is a handwritten letter. I have no idea what it says—not because it's in code or a foreign language or anything, but because all I can focus on is the fifty-dollar bill clipped to the top corner.

Chapter Four

"Is it real?" Chris asks.

"Do I look like a counterfeit expert?" I snort as I rub my fingers over the bill. It's new and smooth— not a wrinkle or rip anywhere. "Do *you* think it's real?"

Chris shrugs. "It could be fake, I guess, but why would somebody stick a bogus bill in a cache? It's not like they're gonna get change back."

"Good point. Maybe we should look at the letter."

Chris flips the bill up out of the way and starts to read while I look over his shoulder and follow along.

Dear Geocacher,

I trust I have your attention. The fact that you are reading this letter means you found the first cache at the cemetery and decoded the clues in the obituary. The reward for your sleuthing is this fifty-dollar bill. You can take it and quit, or you can continue with the hunt. I promise it will be worth your while.

However, the challenge I extend to you is not for the faint of heart. Nor is it for lazy thinkers. From here on out, there's no more GPS. You're going to have to use your geo-senses. If you're clever enough, resourceful enough and daring enough, you won't be disappointed.

You will have three days to find two more caches and present yourself at the finish line. Three days—that's all. After that, the game is over. The clock is ticking. Good luck.

"It sounds like *Mission Impossible*," I say.

"Yeah, it does," Chris agrees. "Let's hope the fifty doesn't self-destruct."

We both grin. Then I nod toward the letter. "So what's our mission?"

Chris starts to read again.

Follow the marathon man. Hurry northwest before flying south. Remember, this isn't a picnic. Billy loves Sara. Be prepared for danger and be on edge. Good luck finding your nest egg.

"That's the clue?"

Chris shrugs. "Apparently. What do you think it means?"

"Absolutely nothing!" I hoot. "It's just a bunch of goofy sentences strung together. Whoever wrote that is messing with our heads."

"Maybe not. We didn't see the clue in the obituary right away either. Besides, if the puzzle was easy to figure out, it wouldn't be a challenge."

"Oh, this is a challenge, all right."

"Don't give up before we've even started." Chris taps the fifty-dollar bill. "If we find the next cache, there could be more money. Maybe a freakin' truckload of money. Do you want someone else to get it?"

"Okay, fine," I concede. "I guess we don't have anything to lose. The fifty bucks is ours to keep no matter what."

Chris grins and slaps me on the back. "Exactly." Then his face gets serious again. "So let's start with *marathon man*. What do you think that means?"

"It's an old movie," I say, without even having to think. When Chris eyeballs me like I'm missing a few brain cells, I add, "My parents have the DVD."

"What's it about?"

"Just because it's in my house doesn't mean I've watched it."

Chris nods. "Right. So what other possibilities are there? Maybe there's a real-life marathon man." Suddenly his eyes light up like someone has flipped on a switch in his head. "What about that Simon Whitfield guy? He came to our school. Remember? He's a marathon man, isn't he? And he lives in Victoria."

I shake my head. "He's a triathlete. It's not the same thing."

Chris frowns. "Too bad. I thought I was on to something." He sighs. "Never mind. It doesn't matter. We'll figure it out. So what about the *Hurry northwest before flying south*? I'm thinking that's gotta be directions."

"Yeah, probably. But northwest from where? And when are we supposed to head south?"

Chris's eyes narrow. "I bet you anything there's a trick in there. The person who hid the caches doesn't waste words. They all mean something. So *Hurry* and *fly* are probably part of the clue too."

"Brilliant deduction," I say. "But that doesn't get us any closer to figuring out the clue. The only part that makes any sense at all is the bit about this not being a picnic. No kidding! But who the heck are Billy and Sara? And what do they have to do with the search?"

Chris shakes his head. "I don't know. But I have a feeling this cache isn't going to be easy to get to, even when we figure out where it is."

"Why do you say that?"

"The letter says we have to be daring, it says the search isn't going to be a picnic, and it stresses that it's dangerous."

"So do you still want to do it?" I say.

"Oh yeah! This is the most fun I've had all year! And if there's money to be had, even better. Bring it on, man."

"*If* there's money. All the letter says is that finding the other two caches will be worth our while. It doesn't say we're going to get money. We're just assuming we will because of the fifty-dollar bill."

"Not only that," Chris argues. "The letter says *Good luck finding your nest egg*. A nest egg is a person's savings."

"Maybe," I say, "or maybe it means the next cache is going to be an egg again, and it's going to be hidden in a nest."

Chris frowns. "Don't be so negative. Are you with me on this thing or aren't you?"

I frown back. "Of course I am. I'm just saying we shouldn't jump to conclusions. Until we decipher the clues, our search isn't going anywhere. And so far we've got nothing."

Chris waves away my concerns. "Don't worry. We'll figure it out."

I roll my eyes. "Yeah, right. And what about this cache?" I wave the metal tube. "We have to put it back." Noting the horrified look on Chris's face, I add, "Without the money."

"Why bother? Do you really think anyone else is going to come looking for it? And even if they do, what are they going to think when there's no fifty bucks attached?"

"To tell you the truth, I don't care. I just think we should stick to the geocaching rules." I can tell Chris is getting ready to protest, but I don't give him the chance. "I wouldn't feel right if we took the cache with us— and neither would you. You're the one who's always going on about following the rules. That shouldn't change just because there could be money involved. So just take a picture of the letter, and boost me back up to the knothole."

Chapter Five

When he gets home, Chris sends me a copy of the clue from his phone, and right after supper I go to my room to try to decipher it. Yeah, right! I can't make any sense of the words no matter how hard I stare at them. At first that only frustrates me, but after a while I start to panic. Chris and I have three days to find the other two caches.

Two of those days are going to be eaten up by school, so there isn't much time.

Then I have a thought. How would the person who wrote the letter know when Chris and I found the cache? How could he or she know when to start counting down the days? Someone had to have been at the hospital watching us. Either that or…

I turn on my computer and navigate to the geocaching website. Maybe there was a time limit on this cache that I didn't notice this morning. I follow the chain of links to the listing.

Except, there is no listing.

I scroll through all the posts. I check the other categories too. Nothing. The listing has vanished. How can that be? It was brand-new this morning.

I scowl at the computer screen like *it* somehow made the listing disappear. The longitude and latitude coordinates *were* there. I didn't imagine them.

I got them from the website, and they led to the cache in the cemetery. And the clues in that cache took us to the one at the hospital. Both caches were very real. So was the fifty-dollar bill.

None of this is making any sense. A listing goes up and comes down on the very same day. Who would do that? And why? It was up for such a short time, Chris and I are probably the only ones who had a chance to look for the caches.

Ding, ding, ding! Suddenly, bells start ringing in my brain.

I smack my forehead with the heel of my hand. Of course! Maybe Chris and I are the only ones who are *supposed* to look for the caches. I don't mean that they were hidden especially for us. But maybe they were only meant to be found once, which means Chris and I are probably the only ones in the hunt.

At first I like that idea. If there's no competition, the fifty dollars is ours, and so is anything else we find. But the more I think about it, the more I feel like a fish on a hook. Chris and I are playing this game blind. Who knows where this chase is going to take us? We could be getting sucked in royally.

Acting on a hunch, I tear out to the carport and hop onto my bike. In ten minutes, I'm back at the cemetery. I stash my bike behind a bush and head up the path toward the spot where Chris and I found the first cache. But as I approach it, I see someone kneeling by the grave. I duck behind the same tree we hid behind earlier.

I wait for my heart to start beating normally again, and then I peer around the tree trunk. It's a woman crouched by the grave, and she's all covered up. Even though it's a warm May evening, she's in baggy sweats. She's wearing a hat and sunglasses too. The only part of her that's showing is her hands.

She's digging into the bouquet. When she lifts her head and glances around, I pull back behind the tree. Once again my heart is pounding in my chest.

When I think it's safe, I poke my head out on the other side of the tree. The woman is still kneeling. I can see the cache in her hands. Did she discover it by accident? Or did she come looking for it? Maybe she hid it, and now that the listing has been withdrawn, she has come to take it away.

I watch her open the yellow-and-white box. The first thing she pulls out is the ticket stub to the dance. She stares at it for a few seconds before flipping it over. Finally, she stuffs it into a jacket pocket and fishes out the obituary.

She sits down on the grass and reads it. She's facing me, and even though she's wearing sunglasses, I can tell she's frowning.

She must sit there, staring at the obituary, for a good five minutes. Finally, her face relaxes, and she sticks the obituary and box into her pocket and pushes herself to her feet. Then she smiles, pats the headstone and heads off down the path.

I wait until I figure she's good and gone before I leave my hiding spot. I go to the grave. I don't know why. There's nothing it can tell me now.

I check out the bouquet. With the cache gone, it's just a bunch of flowers and ribbons, and the grave is just a grave. It's like a hot link in a computer game that goes dead once you've found what you need.

I stand up, but instead of heading back to my bike, I start down the path the woman took. It's empty, but I can see a car parked on the road below. And then I blink, and the woman walks out of the trees and back onto the trail.

I stop breathing. Out of the corner of my eye, I see her turn in my direction. But that's all I see, because I'm already tearing back to my bike.

"Who was it?" Chris asks when I call to tell him what happened.

"I don't know!" I shout into the phone. I'm still rattled by the thought that the woman might have seen my face.

"It was a lady. That's all I can tell you."

"Old? Young? Fat? Skinny?"

"All of the above. None of the above. I don't know. She was wearing a sweat suit, a hat and dark glasses."

"It was probably the bride. If anybody knew there was a cache in the bouquet, it would be her."

"I guess," I say. "But what do you think about the listing being pulled from the website?"

"I think it's great!" Chris says. "If there's no competition, our chances of winning are excellent."

"Competition or not, we're not going to win if we can't figure out the clues," I remind him.

"No problem," Chris drawls. I can't believe how confident he sounds.

"I hope that means you've had better luck figuring out the clues than I have," I say.

"Not all of them," he admits, though he still sounds pretty smug. "But enough to get us going. And I'm pretty sure the rest of it will start to make sense as we go along."

"Explain, please," I say as my hopes start to rise again.

Chris chuckles. "Let's just say that tomorrow is going to be a long day. Pack a lunch and make sure your bike is ready for a good ride. I'll be at your house at nine sharp."

"Why? What are we—" I begin, but Chris has already hung up.

Chapter Six

"The Sooke Potholes! Are you crazy?
Do you know how far that is?"

Chris shrugs. "That depends on where
you start and what route you take."

I wheel my bike out of the carport.
"Well, we're obviously starting here, so
no matter what route we take, Sooke is
a long way."

"True, but we're not traveling by road. We're going to go as the crow flies." He snickers. "Well, more like as the goose flies."

I glare at him. "You're starting to sound like that stupid letter. Crow flies, goose flies. Why not horseflies? What the heck are you talking about?"

Chris laughs again. "Relax, Eric. It's a play on words—like in the letter. Whoever wrote those clues likes double meanings. You know—to get us thinking one thing when we should be thinking something else. But I'm starting to catch on."

"Well, I'm not. So help me out. And start at the beginning."

Chris nods. "Okay. Yesterday, when I got home, I started thinking about the clues in both caches. The first one was connected to Richard Carlisle—that dead guy in the cemetery. It made me wonder if the second one was too. So I looked him up on the Internet."

In my mind, I kick myself for not thinking to do the same thing. But all I say out loud is, "So what did you find?"

"Mostly information about his business, but also that he was a big humanitarian. He gave money to all kinds of charities, sponsored kids in Third World countries, stuff like that. His wife died a few years ago. His only living relative is his daughter, Jane. I'm thinking she was the bride we saw at the cemetery. I also found out that Carlisle was an outdoorsy guy who spent a lot of summers hiking and camping in the Sooke River Canyon. He was a distance runner too. He ran the Victoria Marathon every year, right up to the time he got sick. And his favorite training route was the Galloping Goose Trail." Chris wiggles his eyebrows. "Are you starting to get the picture?"

The first clue from the letter flashes across my brain. *Follow the marathon man.* It looks like that would be Richard Carlisle. I think about the next clue. *Hurry northwest before flying south.*

"What direction is the Galloping Goose Trail from Victoria?" I ask Chris.

His face breaks into a big grin. "I knew you'd catch on! It's northwest."

I smile too. "And it leads to the Sooke River Canyon and the Potholes."

"Bingo."

I nod. "Okay, but I still don't get the *flying south* bit?"

"I think it's just another way of telling us to take the Galloping Goose trail. You know—because geese fly south."

"Yeah," I say. "So you think the next cache is in Sooke?"

"Yup."

I slap Chris on the back and strap on my helmet. "So what are we waiting for? Let's go."

The Galloping Goose was once a railway line, but now it's a trail for hikers and cyclists. Parts of it are paved, others aren't. From downtown Victoria to Leechtown, which is past the Sooke Potholes, the trail is fifty-five kilometers long.

Chris and I get on at Atkins Road, which shortens our ride a lot. It's still a long way, though, and it takes all morning for us to get to the Potholes.

It's a sunny day, so there are lots of people on the trail—joggers, skaters, families with strollers and dogs, and other cyclists. There are lots of girls, too, and some of them are pretty hot. But Chris and I are on a mission. We don't have time for sightseeing. As we get into the more wooded areas, the pavement turns to gravel and hard-packed dirt, and the crowds thin out. Now it's mostly hikers, a few cyclists and the occasional horse and rider.

After rattling over a wooden bridge, Chris and I pull over to the side of the trail for a water break.

I take a long swig from my water bottle and then wipe my forehead with my arm. I squint up at the sun. It's starting to get hot. "How much farther do you think?" I say. "My legs have turned to spaghetti, and my butt is numb."

"I don't know," Chris replies. "But we have to be getting close. Maybe we should figure out the rest of the clues." He rattles them off like he's a tape recorder. *"Remember, this isn't a picnic. Billy loves Sara. Be prepared for danger and be on edge. Good luck finding your nest egg."*

"Well, if the clue writer is sticking to a pattern, all those things are going to come up in that order," I tell him.

Chris looks at me, puzzled. "What do you mean?"

"Think about it. Nothing so far has been mixed up. All the pieces of the longitude and latitude coordinates in the obituary were listed in the right order. We didn't have to rearrange them. And the first two clues from the letter have been in order too." I shrug. "I'm just sayin'."

Chris frowns for a second. Finally, he mutters, "You're right. I should have thought of that."

I take another swig of water to hide my smile. Chris is a smart guy, so whenever I get one past him, I feel like I've won an Olympic medal.

"So you think *this isn't a picnic* is coming up next?" he says.

I bob my head. "Yeah."

Chris gets back on his bike. "Okay, then. I guess we keep our eyes open for something that screams picnic."

That something appears around the next bend. Not only does it scream at us, it practically jumps onto the trail.

This part of the Galloping Goose is totally owned by Mother Nature. It's a forest. On one side, the trees go on forever. On the other side, they come and go in clumps. They disappear completely sometimes, and that's when you realize you're near the edge of a cliff.

It's like that when we round the bend. The trees on one side suddenly vanish, exposing a clearing between the forever-blue sky and the rushing water and rocks of the Sooke River.

And right in the middle of the clearing is a picnic table.

Chris and I spot it at the same time and race straight for it. You'd think we'd found the pot of gold at the end of the rainbow.

"This has to be the place," Chris says, throwing down his bike. I can tell he's excited.

I am too. "So what now?" I pant.

"*Billy loves Sara.*"

Suddenly the clue makes sense. "I bet you anything that's carved somewhere on the table," I say.

But it isn't. Chris and I look everywhere, but all that's scratched into the wood is a lightning bolt and the name of a band.

"I was so sure there would be a lover's heart carved into the table," I sigh.

"There's not," Chris says as he stands up and starts walking toward the cliff.

"You don't need to get suicidal about it," I say. But when Chris keeps on walking, I add, "Hey, man, be careful. It's dangerous over there."

It's like he doesn't hear me. When he finally does turn back to look at me, he's smiling. I think he's gone goofy, but he points and says, "It's carved in this tree."

I look past him, and sure enough, there's a heart chiseled into the tree trunk. Inside it are the words *Billy loves Sara.* I move in for a closer look, though I keep one eye on the cliff. The tree is awfully close to the edge, and I'm not good with heights.

"*Be prepared for danger and be on edge.*" Chris's voice sounds fuzzy and far away.

He takes another step toward the cliff. Now he's standing right on the edge. And he's looking down. I get dizzy just watching him.

"Hey, Eric. Look." Now Chris is pointing down at something. "This is it."

It takes all the nerve I have to move closer, but I do. I don't want Chris to think I'm chicken. Now I'm looking over the edge too. My stomach is churning.

"See it?" Chris says.

Sweat is dripping into my eyes, but I make myself focus. About three meters below the cliff we're standing on is another cliff, and growing on it—practically straight out over the edge—is a small tree. It looks more like a branch than a tree. My thigh is fatter than it is. I look along the trunk. At the end is a nest. No bird though. Instead, there's a toy lantern. And even from here, I can see there's something inside the lantern.

Chris turns toward me and grins. "Looks like we've found our nest egg."

Chapter Seven

"Yeah," I say, but I'm not the least bit excited. Mostly I'm terrified about standing on the edge of the cliff, so I back away and head for the clearing. My knees are shaking so much, they barely hold me up. When I reach the table, they give out altogether, and I collapse onto the bench.

Chris doesn't notice. I might not be thrilled about the cache, but he is. He's jacked enough for both of us. He doesn't seem to realize there's no way we can get to it. It might as well be on the moon.

When he comes back to the table, he's practically dancing. He swoops down onto the bench across from me. Then he slouches out of his backpack and heaves it onto the table.

"We've found it!" he grins.

"Yeah, but we still have to get it. And that could be a problem. Maybe you didn't notice, but the tree it's in is hanging out over the middle of nowhere. And it doesn't look that sturdy. There's no way we can climb out onto it." The thought of trying makes my world spin.

Chris waves away my concerns. "You worry too much."

"Ha!" I hoot as a man and woman on bikes ride into the clearing. They look in our direction for a half second and then continue along the trail.

Chris lowers his voice and pats his pack. "I brought a rope."

"How's that going to help?" I scoff. "You think you can lasso that lantern?"

Chris frowns. "Don't be a jerk. I'm gonna use the rope to climb down the cliff." He pauses. "Or you are. One of us is. It's my rope, but I'll flip you to see who gets to use it."

"That's crazy! *You're* crazy! Climb down the cliff and onto that skinny branch? That's suicide."

Chris shrugs. "Not with the rope as backup."

My jaw drops open. "You *are* crazy. There's no way I'm climbing down there."

Chris looks puzzled. "You sure? You're gonna let me have all the fun? You don't even want to flip me for it?"

I shake my head. "No way." I have no intention of confessing my phobia, but my mouth turns traitor on me anyway, and I blurt out, "I can't do heights."

Right away, I wish I could take the words back. Chris will think I'm a total wimp.

"Seriously?" he says.

I nod and look away. "I can barely look out over the cliff, never mind climb down it. Just thinking about it makes me want to puke."

I expect Chris to laugh, but he only says, "Then you'll have to take care of things up here while I climb down."

The next thing I know, we're tying one end of the rope around the *Billy loves Sara* tree and the other around Chris, and he's getting set to head down the cliff.

He tugs on the rope to make sure it's secure. Then he starts lowering himself over the edge, letting out the rope a little at a time.

I watch from the safety of the tree until Chris's head disappears.

"Okay," he calls up after a few seconds. "I'm on the ledge. Now I'm going to shinny out to the end of the tree. Can you keep an eye on it and tell me if it looks like it's gonna break?"

I take a step toward the edge of the cliff and then stop. I'm not even looking down yet, and already I feel dizzy. I swallow hard and reach back for the tree.

"Eric? You there, man?"

I swallow again. "Yeah. I'm coming."

But my feet are frozen to the spot.

Afraid of heights or not, I can't leave Chris out there on that skimpy branch without even a lookout. I drop to the ground and crawl commando style to the edge of the cliff. My hands grip the sharp, rocky ledge while my runners wedge toeholds in the dirt. Only when I feel like my body is glued to the earth do I look over the edge.

All I see is the water crashing over the rocks far below. The sound of it fills my ears, and my vision starts to swirl. I feel like I'm being dragged down a bathtub drain. I shut my eyes and wait for the spinning to stop.

"You okay?" Chris says. "You look awful white."

"I'm fine," I lie. I block out the river and focus on Chris. "Have you tested your weight on the tree?"

He moves his head. I think he's nodding, but it's hard to tell from this angle.

"It's stronger than it looks," he says. "I think it's going to be fine, but yell if you see it start to move."

It's my turn to nod. "Be careful," I tell him.

He doesn't answer. He climbs onto the tree and starts shinnying up and out. I imagine I hear the trunk crack and see it break, dumping Chris into the river. I shake off the image and stare at the tree.

I look at the rope, angling down over my shoulder from the tree behind me. It's stretched as far as it can go. I steal a quick glance at Chris. He's stretched too—flat along the length of the tree, his arm reaching toward the nest. His fingers claw at it, trying to pull it closer.

I hold my breath and will the tree to be strong. The rope groans as Chris tries to shinny out a bit farther. I hear a scraping noise behind me, and suddenly the rope that was taut above me is right on top of me. It digs into my shoulder and pins me to the ground. The rope has slid down the trunk of the *Billy loves Sara* tree.

Horrified, I look down. Chris is gone. My stomach leaps into my mouth, and the rocks and rushing river below become a blur. *Oh, God. Don't let this be happening.*

"Chris!" I scream. "Chris! Where are you? Chris, answer me!" The rope is really cutting into me. I know it will jerk again if I wriggle out from under it, but if I stay where I am, it's going to take my shoulder off. Besides, I need to find Chris. Using my free hand to push at it, I pull my body the other way and slide free. The rope thumps to the ground like a giant elastic being snapped. There is a roar of complaint below. I peer back over the cliff and holler again. "Chris!"

Finally, I see him—his hands, actually—hanging onto the tree, but at least he hasn't fallen into the river. Not yet.

"Chris!" I yell down to him. "Hang on. I'm going to get help."

The words are no sooner out of my mouth than I hear footsteps pounding the ground behind me. Then somebody is pulling me away from the cliff. It's the man and woman who cycled past the clearing earlier.

"What happened?" the man says. "Where's your friend?"

I point down to the ledge. "There."

The man looks over the cliff. "Hang on, kid. I'm coming."

I look down again. Chris is still dangling from the tree, but he's working his way hand over hand to the ledge. Before the guy even begins to climb down, Chris is back on his feet.

He grins and waves. "I'm okay." A couple of minutes later, he has scaled the cliff and is back on solid ground.

Wearing a worried frown, the guy looks Chris over like he expects him to be missing an arm or a leg. "What the heck were you doing down there? You could have been killed."

"I dropped something," Chris says. "So I climbed down to get it."

"And did you?" the woman asks.

"Did I what?"

"Get what you dropped."

Chris lowers his eyes and shakes his head. "Nah. It fell in the river."

Chapter Eight

When the man and woman are convinced Chris is okay, they scold him for being reckless and make him swear not to do anything stupid like that again. Then they get on their bikes and leave.

Chris doesn't seem the least bit shook-up. I can't believe it. If I'd been dangling over the Sooke River on the end of a rope, I would be a wreck.

"I'm glad you're okay," I tell him. "For a couple of minutes there, I thought you were dead."

Chris grins. "Nope. Totally alive, as you can see."

"How can you be so calm? That was really scary. And all for nothing."

"Not really," he drawls. He reaches behind him into the waistband of his jeans and pulls out the toy lantern that had been in the bird's nest.

For a second, I think I'm seeing things. I blink a couple of times. "You got it? But you said it fell into the river."

Chris shrugs. "I had to say that, or those people would have wanted to look at it. And then they would've asked a ton of questions."

"Yeah, you're right," I agree. I slug him in the arm. "So open it!"

As Chris fumbles with the tiny latch, his hands shake. I'm thinking maybe his hanging over the Sooke River got to him more than he wants to let on.

He shoves the lantern at me. "You open it. My fingers are too big and clumsy."

I don't say anything. I just take the lantern.

Opening it is a snap. Digging out the paper that's inside is a whole different matter. It's wedged in so tight, it's hard to get a grip on it.

"Don't rip it," Chris says as I twist and tug.

"I'm not," I snap. "This isn't easy, you know."

Chris doesn't say anything else.

Eventually, I manage to shift the paper enough that I can grab a corner and pull. Chris holds on to the lantern so that I can concentrate on yanking out the paper. Finally, it pops free.

"Open it," he says. He's practically breathing down my neck. I've never seen him so uptight.

"Relax, will ya? I'm going as fast as I can."

When I get the paper unfolded, I smooth it out on the picnic table.

The top half is a comic drawing of an eagle in a nest. It's wearing an army helmet, and it's sitting on a grenade. The dialogue bubble by the eagle's head says, *Sometimes you gotta go out on a limb. Heh, heh, heh.*

"Very funny," Chris sneers. "This guy is a real comedian."

I point to the lower half of the paper. "Read the rest."

Congratulations on locating the third cache. Even more important,

*congratulations on retrieving it.
Obviously, you enjoy a challenge. That's
good, because finding the last cache is
going to be even tougher. Good luck.*

Time to move forward.

After that comes the clue. At least,
I think it's a clue.

—*gj22f-tje5e 16sp10fd20jpo 15o 1
gp18ujg9dbujpo*

—*hfp13fusj3 gjhvsf 23jui gpvs
f17vb12 19usbj7iu tj4ft boe 6p21s sjh8u
b14hmft*

"Great," I groan. "Now, before we
can even try to figure out what the clue
means, we have to figure out what it
says. How's your Russian?"

"That's not Russian," Chris scoffs.

"Well, it sure as heck isn't English."

"Maybe the guy's a really bad
speller."

"I'll say. He doesn't even know his letters from his numbers."

Chris ignores me and goes back to studying the paper. "Obviously, it's some kind of code."

"No kidding," I snort. "The question is, *what* code?"

Without looking up, Chris says, "We'll figure it out."

By the end of school the next day, we still haven't cracked the code.

When I exit the building, I don't see Chris, so I lean against the brick wall near the entrance to wait. The air is an energetic whirr of voices as kids stream past. Two girls look my way and giggle behind their hands. I hope they're laughing at the dorky-looking dude with the briefcase standing beside me. I move to the other side of the entrance and watch a couple of guys toss a football. A long pass bounces off the hood of a red convertible parked at the curb. One of the guys runs into the street to retrieve the football and then says something to the lady behind the wheel.

"Well?" Chris appears out of nowhere and leans against the wall too. "Did you figure it out?"

I shake my head. "Nope. How about you?"

"Uh-uh."

"So now what?"

"We keep thinking."

"We don't have a lot of time, you know. Just one more day. And we're no closer to deciphering the code than we were yesterday."

"We're just missing the key," Chris mumbles, almost to himself.

"We've tried everything."

"No, we haven't," Chris says. "Otherwise, we'd have figured it out."

He whips his copy of the clue out of his pocket and reads it aloud—the part that's readable, that is. "The guy who wrote this is trying to tell us something. He's giving us a clue to cracking the code. I just know it."

"You mean the *time to move forward* bit? Trust me, we're not moving anywhere. Half the code is letters, and the other half is numbers. How are we supposed to figure that out?"

"*Time to move forward*," Chris mutters again. "Why say that? Why not just say, 'Here's the clue'? Time to move forward. Time is numbers, so let's concentrate on that."

"What numbers are in the code?" I dig out a paper and pencil and write them down as Chris rattles them off. "They range from one to twenty-three," I say when I'm done, "but two and eleven are missing. There are no repeats."

"Okay, there are no huge numbers. Nothing bigger than twenty-three. Maybe each number represents a letter. What do you think?"

"But there are twenty-six letters in the alphabet. The highest number is twenty-three."

"So some of the letters are left out. If one equals *a* and so on, the missing letters would be *x*, *y* and *z*. It wouldn't be hard to write a clue without those letters."

I nod and do some fast computing. "The other numbers left out of the code are two and eleven, which would be *b* and *k*. You could probably write a message without those letters too."

"Okay," Chris says, and I can tell he's getting pumped. "Let's rewrite the code, inserting letters for those numbers, and see if it tells us anything."

—*gjvf-tjeee pspjfdtjpo oo a gprujgidbujpo*

—hfpmfusjc gjhvsf wjui gpvs fqvbl susbjgiu tjdft boe fpus sjhhu bnhmft

"It still doesn't make any sense," I say when we're done.

Chris stabs a finger at the paper. "Except for that."

I look where he's pointing. "The letter *a*? What's so big about that?"

"Don't you get it? It's all by itself. It's the word *a*. It has to be."

"Oh, good," I reply sarcastically. "We know one of the words is *a*. We've practically got this thing solved."

Chris doesn't hear me. He's totally focused on figuring out the code. "We got the *time* part. Now we just need to *move forward*. But how?"

That's when a bell goes off in my head. "I got it!" I say. I start to scribble, changing the letters in the first word of the code to the letters that come next alphabetically.

The result is *hkwg-ukff*. I chuck my pencil. "So much for that idea. I thought for sure the code was telling us to move the letters forward."

Chris picks up my pencil and hands it back. "What if the letters have already been moved forward? Maybe we need to move them backward instead."

So I do. *Gjvf-tjeee* now becomes *fiue-siddd*.

Chris sighs and slumps against the wall. "That's no better."

"It does look more like a word," I say. I look at the original code word with numbers and letters. "What if?" I start to scribble again.

"What if what?" Chris peers over my shoulder.

"What if we leave the letters that were originally numbers alone because they've already been changed once?" When I finish writing, I smack the paper with my pencil. "Ta-da! *Five-sided.*

And in case you haven't noticed, that's a real word."

For a second, Chris turns into a statue. He's not blinking. He doesn't even seem to be breathing. Finally, he says, "Hurry up. Decode the rest."

"*Five-sided projection on a fortification,*" I read, and then, "*Geometric figure with four equal straight sides and four right angles.*" I look up. "That second one is a square."

Chris nods. His eyes are glittering. "And the first one is a bastion. I had a toy fort when I was a kid." His face breaks into the biggest grin I've ever seen. "We're going to Bastion Square."

Chapter Nine

Now that we've figured out where the next cache is, Chris and I can't wait to start looking for it. There's a bus stop outside the school, so we hop on a bus for downtown and Bastion Square. We're barely up the steps before the driver shuts the door and pulls away from the curb, so we weave our way down the aisle like a couple of drunks and flop onto the backseat. Then we slouch into opposite corners and stretch out.

Chris chucks a wadded gum wrapper at my head. "This is it," he says. "The last cache, *and* we're a day ahead of schedule. Oh, yeah. We are da men."

"We haven't found the cache yet," I remind him. "Maybe we should hold off celebrating until we actually have it in our hands."

Chris makes a face and waves away my words. "It's in the bag, man."

I shake my head. "Don't be so sure. There could be another twist. The guy who hid the caches has a thing for surprises. Or haven't you noticed?"

"I bet you half your share of the prize that we find that cache today."

"You really think I'm going to take that bet?" I hoot. "You're a moron." I chuck the gum wrapper back at him.

He grins and deflects it with his arm. Then we both sit back and look out the window.

It's almost rush hour, and the bus is entering the city center, so traffic is starting to bog down. When we stop at a light, we're hemmed in on all sides.

Chris whistles. "Take a look at that."

"What?"

"Second car back." He nods toward the line of vehicles behind the bus.

"You mean that red convertible?"

"Yeah, that *and* the girl inside."

"What's so special about her? You can't even see her," I say. "Her hair is covered with a scarf, and she's wearing sunglasses."

"She's hot," Chris insists.

I start to laugh.

Chris frowns. "What's so funny?"

"I was just thinking how dumb you're going to feel when you find out that that girl is the mom of a kid we go to school with."

He kicks my foot. "She is not."

I kick him back. "There was a red convertible parked outside the school today. And the driver was a lady. Could've been this car and this lady. Most ladies in cars parked outside of schools are moms." I pause before adding, "But if that's your thing—" I grin and move my legs before he can kick me again.

We get off the bus at Douglas Street and hang a right onto View. After a couple of blocks, we're in the tourist part of downtown. We cross Government Street with the Bastion Square entrance straight ahead. There is a glass and metal archway with the name welded onto it. The huge building on our right is a pub, according to the sign, but it looks like it could have been a bank once. Like all the other old buildings around here, it's kept in good shape to attract the tourists.

From this point on, it's foot traffic only. No cars are allowed in Bastion Square. Good thing, too. There's no room for them. The place is swarming with pedestrians.

Chris and I walk down one side of the square to the Wharf Street boundary, then up the other side toward Langley Street, where we slide onto a bench just vacated by a couple of old guys.

"Did you see it?" Chris asks.

He means the cache. I *didn't* see it, but something in his voice makes me think he might have, so I turn quickly to look at him. "Did you?"

He shakes his head. "Where do you think it could be?"

"Not in any of the buildings. The rules say it's got to be outside some-where. In the shrubs, maybe, or taped to the bottom of one of the benches?

Over the top of a door or window? It's so wide open here. There aren't a lot of good hiding places. Of course, it would help if we knew what we're looking for."

Chris squints up at the sun and then scans the tops of the buildings.

"Don't tell me you think it's going to be somewhere up there," I say as my stomach does a flip. If I can't climb down a ten-foot cliff, I sure as heck can't scale a fifty-foot wall.

Chris shrugs. "I don't know. Like you said, there aren't a lot of good hiding places around here. I'm just thinking about the possibilities."

"Maybe there's a clue in the note to narrow things down," I say.

"Like what?"

Chris pulls out the paper and we study it, looking for anything that might be a hint. If there is a clue, we don't see it. As we continue to ponder where the cache might be, Chris absentmindedly refolds the paper until it looks like it did when we pulled it out of the lantern.

That makes me wonder if the lantern is the clue. I dig through my backpack and haul it out. I can't quite close my hand around it, but it's still pretty small. The frame and pointed top are black, and it has four clear-plastic panels. One of them is hinged with a latch.

Chris looks at the lantern and then holds the folded paper next to it. "I don't know how that paper ever fit inside," he says.

I spin it in the air. "No kidding, eh? It's kind of a cool little thing though— just like the lanterns here in the square, only miniature."

It takes a few seconds for my words to bore into Chris's brain, but when they do, he jumps up. "That's it! The cache is on one of the lampposts!"

A few people pivot and stare at him like he's some kind of lunatic.

"Shut your hole, man," I shush him. "Do you want the entire world to hear?"

Chris sits down again. "Sorry."

We keep our mouths closed and our butts planted on the bench until we think people have lost interest in us and moved on. Then we take another stroll around the square, checking out all the lamp standards.

"There it is," I hiss. "That lamppost straight ahead. See it? There's a small bag tied to the base of the lantern."

"Got it," Chris says quietly. He keeps walking. Even I can't tell that he looked.

We walk out of Bastion Square. When we're a safe distance away, I say, "I can get up that pole easy. It'll be like climbing rope in gym class."

"I thought you were afraid of heights," Chris says.

"The lamppost isn't high. I could jump down."

Chris nods. "Okay, then. The question is, when? We can't let anybody see us."

I nod. "Right, but with all the restaurants and pubs around there, the square won't quiet down till after one in the morning, I bet."

"Then that's when we'll come back," Chris says as we head to the bus stop.

"Hey, look." I point as we pass a parking lot. "There's that red convertible again. Wanna check it out?"

But Chris doesn't hear me. His mind is focused on that last cache.

Chapter Ten

Chris and I decide to meet behind Broadmead Shopping Center at 1:30 AM. I'll never be able to lie in bed for three and a half hours without falling asleep, so I set the alarm on my watch and pray that nobody else hears it. I guess I doze off with my finger near the snooze button, because the alarm doesn't even sound a full beep before I shut it off and jump out of bed. I am instantly awake and within minutes fully dressed. I arrange the pillows under the blankets to look like a body, and then I'm gone. The sneaking-out part is easy. My room is in the basement, and there's a door leading out to the carport.

At Broadmead, Chris is waiting in the bushes. I'm not expecting him to be there, so when he jumps out, I nearly pee my pants.

We head onto Quadra Street, a straight route into town. During the day, it's a really busy road. Now it's so dead, I'm wondering if Victoria has been taken over by aliens and all the people have been beamed up into space. The streets are so empty, we don't even bother stopping at traffic lights. But we keep an eye out for cars. The last thing we need is to meet up with a cop. Whenever we see head-lights or hear an engine, we pull over into the shadows and wait for the vehicle to pass.

Downtown Victoria is pretty much a ghost town too. Just the same, Chris and I stick to the side streets and alleys. Near Bastion Square, we pass the parking lot where we saw the red convertible that afternoon. It's still there, but now its top is up and it's parked in a corner.

"Hey," I whisper to Chris and point. "There's your car."

He looks and nods. "The lady who was driving it must've been partying. Probably took a cab home. Smart. Still, I don't think I'd want to leave a sweet ride like that sitting in an open parking lot overnight. It could get wrecked or stolen. She's taking a big chance."

"You wanna check it out?"

I can tell by the way Chris hesitates that he's tempted. But he shakes his head and says, "We can do it on the way home. After we get the cache."

We leave our bikes near the entrance to Bastion Square and slip into a dark doorway. Though it's the middle of the night, the streetlamps shed a lot of light, and we can't take the chance of being seen. We scan the square to make sure we're alone.

We're not.

On one of the benches across the courtyard is a bag lady with her cart. She looks like she's sleeping.

"Great!" Chris mutters. "If she stays there all night, we're never going to be able to get the cache."

"Maybe we can scare her away," I suggest. "You know—make a noise so she thinks someone is coming."

"What kind of noise?"

"I don't know. Drop something, maybe, or smack something against the wall."

Chris nods. "Good idea. Wait here and watch her."

Chris creeps back to the corner of the building, hauls a flashlight out of his backpack and bangs it against a metal drainpipe. The clanging echoes throughout the square, and I worry that it might do more than wake up the bag lady. All we need is for a security guard to come running. I glance around nervously.

"Well?" Chris says as he slides back into the doorway beside me.

I look toward the bench. "I think it worked. She's awake, anyway."

As we watch, the woman gets up, grabs her cart and shuffles slowly out of the courtyard, dissolving into the shadows.

We take one last look around before hurrying to the cache.

"It's still there," Chris whispers. "You ready? Want a boost?" Before I can answer, he cups his hands together and braces them on his leg.

I rub my hands up and down my jeans. I don't want to slip. Then I grab the post, step into the foothold Chris has made and wrap my body around the pole. I slide my knees up and grip the slippery metal with the tread of my runners, reach for a higher grip with my hands and then straighten my legs. I repeat the process a few more times. My gaze is glued to the little leather pouch tied to the base of the lantern. Near the top of the pole, I lose my grip and slide down a few centimeters, but my runners act as a brake, and I'm able to pull myself back up.

It's a good thing I'm not a huge guy, because once I've climbed the post as far as I can, I have to support my entire weight with my feet and one arm. I need the other arm to undo the pouch. And, of course, the drawstring is tied in a knot.

"Hurry up," Chris whispers.

That startles me, and I almost lose my grip. "Is somebody coming?" Now I'm sweating, so I rub my hands on my jeans again. First one, then the other.

"No," Chris calls back, "but they probably will be soon. Snap it up."

"I'm going as fast as I can," I growl. I peer around the square to make sure no one is around. If nothing else, I have a good view. I'm about to get working on the knot again when a movement in the shadows makes me stop. I peer harder into the darkness, but I don't see anything. I give my head a shake and look again. Nothing. I must be seeing things.

It's hard to untie the knot with one hand. The pouch keeps twisting around the pole. This would be much easier if I had a knife.

"Are you nearly done?" It's Chris again.

"A couple more secs," I grunt as I grab the runaway bag for the fiftieth time. I have an idea. I hold the pouch still with my teeth. That makes it way easier to work on the knot. The drawstring is made of leather, so it's not hard to get a grip. Right away, I feel the knot start to give. Once I get it going, it comes undone easily. In less than a minute I have the pouch unfastened.

"Comin' down," I say. In one motion, I grab the bag and slide down the lamppost.

"What's in it?" Chris demands before my feet have even touched the ground.

I dangle the pouch in front of him. "You think I've got X-ray vision?"

He grabs the pouch and loosens the drawstring, and now suddenly I'm the one who's impatient.

"It's a business card," he says. "DeGroot, Jamieson & Associates, attorneys at law. Lawyers? I don't want to get mixed up with freakin' lawyers."

"Wait. Turn it over. There's something written on the back."

Chris flips the card and squints at the writing.

"What does it say?"

"*Congratulations! You have found the final cache. Bring this card to my office before 5 PM tomorrow to claim your reward.* It's signed by a Martin Jamieson."

Chris looks at me and I look at him. It takes a few seconds for the reality of what's happening to sink in. Finally, Chris grabs both my arms—tightly— and starts shaking me.

"This is it!" he says. "We've done it. We've found all the caches. All we have to do now is collect our prize. Woo-hoo! Tomorrow we're gonna be rich." He's not whispering anymore.

I'm excited, too, but I don't want to risk blowing everything, so I shush him and start pulling him toward our bikes. I take the business card from him and look at it more closely.

"This Jamieson guy's office is on Douglas Street. We can catch a bus after school and be there by four o'clock." I look at my watch. "But now we have to get home. If my parents find out I've been riding all over Victoria in the middle of the night, I won't live to see tomorrow."

We hop on our bikes and head back the way we came. Chris is so high, I swear he could fly home. As we pass the parking lot, I look for the red convertible, but it's gone. All that's there now is a wire cart.

Chapter Eleven

It's three thirty in the morning when I sneak back into the house. After being up for twenty hours and cycling to town and back, I should be dead tired. But I'm too pumped. Chris and I found all the caches—and they were *not* easy to find, so I'm totally stoked about that. But even better, now we get a prize. Someone is actually going to reward us for doing what we like to do. My heart is beating faster than a hummingbird's wings, and so many thoughts are whirring around in my head, it's impossible to think them all. How can I sleep?

Suddenly, my stomach growls— really loud. It sounds like some kind of animal is trapped in there. All that riding has made me hungry. Luckily, I have half a candy bar in my backpack. I dig it out and wolf it down. So now I'm on a sugar high too.

Needless to say, I don't close my eyes all night, but it doesn't matter. When morning arrives, I'm not the least bit tired. In fact, exhaustion doesn't hit me until lunchtime, but boy, does it hit me! One minute I'm walking on air, the next it's like I've been run over by a brigade of steamrollers. I can barely stand. Eating gets rid of the shakes, but it makes me even more tired. I sleep through my afternoon classes.

At three thirty, Chris is waiting for me outside the school.

He frowns when he sees me. "You look like crap, man."

"I don't function well without sleep," I mumble.

Chris grins. "I didn't sleep last night either. Who cares? Shake it off. There'll be plenty of time for sleep after we collect our money." Then he shoves me toward the sidewalk. "So let's go get it."

His enthusiasm is contagious, and I perk up on the bus ride downtown.

"How can you be sure we're going to get money?" I ask him. "How do you know it won't be movie passes or gift certificates or something like that?"

"Easy. We got fifty bucks for finding the first two caches, and they weren't even challenging or dangerous. So the last two have to be worth more." He shakes his head. "Think about it, Eric. Gift certificates for risking our lives? No way, man. It's gotta be money."

The law firm is on the other side of the street, a block from the bus stop. As we wait for the light to change, I stare at the buildings across the street.

"Which one is it?" I wonder out loud.

Chris looks again at the address on the business card and then squints across the street and points. "Second entrance from the corner. The tall sand-colored building."

When the light turns red, we race across the intersection, but as soon as we reach the building, we stop. This is it, and, though it's the moment we've been waiting for, something holds us back. The unknown, I guess. Finally Chris reaches for the door handle and breathes so deeply, I swear he sucks in half the air in Victoria. Then he opens the door, and we're on the move again.

DeGroot, Jamieson & Associates is on the ninth floor, so we take the elevator. Thankfully, it's not one of those glass ones. If I could see how high we're going, I'd probably pass out. The elevator is fast, and only a couple of seconds after the doors close, they open again. Giant lettering on the wall ahead informs us that we've reached the ninth floor. Too bad my stomach is still in the lobby.

Chris scans the directory and then heads left. I follow him. He points to a set of carved wooden doors at the end of the hall, where it splits right and left. "That's it," he says.

The words are no sooner out of his mouth than a woman appears around the corner and walks toward us. She's young and pretty, and the yellow dress she's wearing lights up the dark corridor like sunshine. But it's her hair that I can't stop staring at. It's long and blond and shiny, and it ripples over her shoulders like she's in a shampoo commercial.

She's looking straight at us, and as she gets closer, she smiles. That's when I realize I know her. Well, not actually know her, but I've seen her before. I just don't know where.

She stops in front of us, so we stop too.

"Hi there," she says brightly. "Can I help you fellas?"

Chris smiles at her. He's a sucker for pretty girls. I'm still trying to figure out how I know her.

He shows the woman the business card. "We're looking for DeGroot, Jamieson & Associates," he says, though the office is right in front of us.

The woman lifts Chris's hand so she can see the back of the card. That's when she gasps and covers her mouth.

She takes a step backward. Then she sort of staggers and starts laughing. "You're our mystery treasure hunters!" She points to the business card. "And if you have Martin's card, you've found all the caches. We didn't think anyone would. That's wonderful!"

Before I realize what's happening, she's hugging us, and I can't help noticing how good her hair smells.

When she lets go, she's still smiling. "I'm so glad I ran into you both, because it just so happens I have your reward."

"No kidding," Chris grins.

She nods. "Yes." She fans herself with her hand. "*Whew.* All this excitement is making me hot." She grabs her hair and lifts it off her neck.

Bam! I remember how I know her.

She opens her purse and pulls out a wad of bills.

Chris's eyes practically bulge out of his head.

"Three hundred dollars," she beams. "And it's all yours."

Chris reaches for the money, but the woman pulls it away.

"All you have to do is give me Martin Jamieson's business card."

Chris holds out the card, and the woman holds out the money. Before they can make the exchange, I grab the business card.

Chris scowls at me. "What are you doin', man?"

I shake my head and start walking toward the doors at the end of the hall. "The instructions say to give the card to Martin Jamieson," I remind him. "And that's what we're going to do."

I can hear Chris running to catch up. He grabs my arm. "We don't have to. This lady has our money."

I jerk free of his grip and continue walking.

The woman calls to us. "I'm authorized to increase the reward by two hundred dollars." It could be my imagination, but she sounds anxious.

Chris steps in front of me. "You hear that, Eric? She's offering us five hundred dollars! Give her the freakin' card."

I push him aside and start running, but just as I reach the office, he catches up and tackles me. I don't fall, but we both slam into the doors. Chris tries to wrestle the card out of my hands.

Now the woman has caught up, and she's trying to get the card too.

As I twist and turn, trying to fend them off, I say, "She's trying to con us, Chris! She wants the card so she can collect the reward. Don't you recognize her? She's the woman from—"

That's when the office door bursts open, and the three of us tumble through the opening and land in a heap on the carpet.

A middle-aged man with a mustache so skinny that it looks as if it's been drawn on with a felt marker peers down at us in bewilderment. "Jane?" he says.

Chris sits up and looks first at the man and then at the woman lying on the floor. "Did you say Jane?" he asks. I can tell he's starting to figure things out. "You mean, as in Jane Carlisle?"

The woman disentangles herself, stands up and smooths her dress and hair. "Actually, it's Bartel now."

As Chris slowly nods, I can see a light go on in his brain. "Right," he says. "We were at your wedding."

Chapter Twelve

From behind his desk, Martin Jamieson stares at Chris and me over the top of his glasses. Standing beside him—with arms crossed—is Jane Bartel. She's staring at us too. It's like being in the principal's office. I feel guilty, even though I can't think what Chris and I could have done wrong. Well, unless you count crashing into Jamieson's office and falling on the floor. But Jane did that, too, and she doesn't seem to be in trouble.

Part of me starts to worry that our wrestling match may have cost Chris and me our reward. If we go from five hundred dollars to nothing, it'll be my fault—and Chris will kill me.

I don't know how long Jamieson makes us squirm, but it seems like forever before he clears his throat and pulls a folder out of a drawer.

Let the games begin.

"I wasn't expecting there to be two of you," he says. "And I certainly wasn't expecting you to be so young."

"What difference does that make?" I can tell by Chris's voice that his back is up.

The lawyer frowns. "Perhaps a bit more paperwork, but otherwise, no difference at all. My client made no stipulation as to age or number of claimants."

"So what do we get?" Trust Chris to zip right to the point.

Jamieson clears his throat again. "I'm getting to that. My client is the late Richard Carlisle. He was an independent businessman whose generosity is well-known. He was also an avid geocacher. He—"

Chris practically jumps out of his chair. "That's it! That's how I know his name! I've seen it on geocache logs."

Once again Jamieson clears his throat. "Yes. It was one of his passions—one he shared with his daughter, Jane. In fact, hunting down caches became a competition between them. They often hid their own caches in an effort to outsmart one another." He smiles up at Jane. "They were well-matched."

Then the lawyer turns back to Chris and me. "When he discovered he was dying, Mr. Carlisle decided to plant one last set of caches. These caches were intended to challenge not only Jane, but someone else too." He adjusts his glasses. "The two of you, as it turns out. And the caches were to have an additional incentive."

I have no idea what he's talking about. I look over at Chris to see if he's keeping up, but his face tells me nothing.

"These geocaches would tax the searcher mentally and physically. But because they contained an element of danger, he added a monetary incentive."

"You mean the fifty dollars?" I say. I may not understand lawyer talk, but I do know money.

He nods. "Initially, yes. Mr. Carlisle created all the caches and hid the second and third ones himself, before he became too sick. It was his wish that the search commence on Jane's wedding day, hence the ceremony at the cemetery.

I posted the coordinates on the geocache website beforehand and took them down again later that day. Mr. Carlisle wanted this to be a closed search—only Jane and one other searcher. Once it was underway, I hid the last cache on the lamppost."

Chris looks at Jane and frowns. "I don't get it. The first cache was in your bouquet. How could you be searching for it if you're the one who hid it?"

"As Martin said, my father and I were very competitive. Since this was the last cache he was ever going to hide for me, he made it as difficult as he could. He knew I'd figure out the clues, so he handicapped me. I had instructions to leave the cache, and I wasn't allowed to look at it for six hours. Though I hid it, I had no idea what was in it until after you fellas were on your way to the second cache.

So not only was I chasing the caches—I had to chase you too."

"That was you I saw at the cemetery, in sweats," I say.

She nods. "I saw you, too, which was good, because then I knew who to look for on the Galloping Goose Trail."

"You were there too?" Chris says. "How did you know where to go?"

Jane laughs. "Same as you. I figured out the clues. Thank goodness you left them in the caches. I actually should have beaten you to the Potholes. I knew exactly where to go. You got lucky on that one. Really lucky, when you consider you could have drowned."

Chris's mouth drops open, and he points at Jane. "It was you! When I was dangling over the cliff, it was you who helped."

"That's what I was trying to tell you in the hall," I say. "When I realized she was the lady from the Potholes,

I knew she had to be after the prize. Why else would she show up in both places? It was too much of a coincidence."

"I was afraid you might recognize me," Jane says, "but I had to risk it. Keeping you from delivering that business card to Martin was my last hope of winning."

"Was that you in the red convertible outside our school too?" I ask.

"Yes."

"How did you know what school we went to?"

"You left a ticket to your school dance in the cemetery cache."

I slap my forehead. "Right. And you followed the bus into town?"

She nods.

"I told you she wasn't anybody's mom," Chris says.

"Pardon?" asks Jane.

I wave Chris away. "It's not important. You followed us to Bastion Square?"

"I did. And when you left within minutes of arriving, I knew you must have spotted the cache. After you took off, I walked around that courtyard for hours and never found it. How did you?"

I grin at her and pull out the little lantern. "This was part of the clue we found at the Potholes."

"I didn't even think to look on the lampposts," Jane says. "But I knew you'd come back once Bastion Square emptied out, so I stuck around."

"We saw your car in a parking lot," Chris says. "Sweet ride."

"Thanks. I like it, though I probably should have chosen something more subtle to tail you with." Then she smiles. "Something more like my Bastion Square disguise."

Chris and I exchange glances. "What disguise?" we say at the same time.

"I was the bag lady sleeping on the bench."

Even Martin Jamieson laughs.

"That was you?" Chris says, and suddenly I remember the cart in the parking lot where the red convertible had been.

Then Jane sighs. "I did my best, but you guys beat me fair and square."

"So now that five hundred dollars is ours?" Chris says.

"I'm afraid that offer is no longer on the table." She looks over at me and shakes her head. "Thanks to your friend here."

My stomach drops into my shoes. I really did screw things up.

"You *should* thank him." Martin Jamieson is smiling big-time. "If you had taken Jane's offer, you would have forfeited the money Richard Carlisle authorized me to give you."

I am relieved. It looks like we're still getting a prize, and from the sound of it, it's more than Jane was offering.

As usual, Chris is a step ahead of me. "How much money are we talking about?"

Martin Jamieson's smile gets even bigger, if that's possible. Jane is grinning from ear to ear too.

"Ten thousand dollars."

"*Ten thousand!*" I repeat the number out loud and then over and over in my head, but it doesn't help. It just doesn't want to sink in.

I look over at Chris. His smile is big enough to cover two people's faces. This geocache search has turned out better than even he expected.

"Hey, Jane," he says. "Can I ask you a question?"

She nods. "Absolutely. Shoot."

"How much would you take for that little red convertible of yours?"

Acknowledgments

Special thanks to my editor, Melanie Jeffs. She's a stickler for details, but that's a good thing. After all, it's the little things that make the difference.